Disney · PIXAR
FINDING DORY

The Unforgettable Joke Book

randomhousekids.com

ISBN 978-0-7364-3611-3

Printed in the United States of America

10 9 8 7 6 5 4 3 2 1

Disney · PIXAR
FINDING DORY

The Unforgettable Joke Book

By Sean Cunningham

Illustrated by the Disney Storybook Art Team

Random House 🏠 New York

What does Dory call a fish with no eyes?

A FSH!

How brave is Dory, rated from one to ten?

SHE'S OFF THE SCALE!

Where will Nemo go to complete his education?

FINISHING SCHOOL!

Did you hear about the fish that lost all its scales?

HE COULDN'T *WEIGHT* ANY LONGER!

What does it say under Nemo's yearbook photo?

CLASS
CLOWN!

Why couldn't Marlin afford a new house?

'CAUSE HE DIDN'T
HAVE *ANEMONE!*

What did Marlin pack Nemo for lunch?

PEANUT BUTTER
AND JELLYFISH.

How did Marlin know that Nemo was lying?

HIS STORY SOUNDED
A LITTLE *FISHY!*

Why doesn't Bailey like to play cards with Destiny?

**BECAUSE SHE'S
A REAL CARD SHARK!**

What's a whale's favorite game?

SWALLOW
THE LEADER!

Why did the shark cross the sea?

TO GET TO THE OTHER *TIDE*!

How did Destiny feel about being released into the ocean?

SHE THOUGHT IT WAS OVER-*WHALE*-MING!

Why are fish so smart?

'CAUSE THEY'RE
ALWAYS IN SCHOOLS!

How does Mr. Ray teach the alphabet?

WITH THE A-B-*SEAS*!

Why did Dory bring seaweed to Mr. Ray's class?

SHE WANTED TO *KELP*!

What sea creatures are cranky and like to be left alone?

HERMIT CRABS!

What did one hermit crab say to the other hermit crab when he stole his home?

"DON'T BE SO *SHELLFISH!*"

What do the hermit crabs use to lift things?

MUSSELS!

How does Marlin talk to his friends?

ON HIS *SHELL* PHONE!

What is the best way to communicate with a fish?

DROP IT A LINE!

Did you hear about Dory's new seafood diet?

**SHE *SEES*
FOOD AND EATS IT!**

What do you call a lobster that bites your rear end?

A BOTTOM-FEEDER!

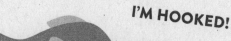

What did the fish say after trying the delicious bait?

I'M HOOKED!

What's the difference between a fish and a piano?

YOU CAN'T *TUNA* FISH!

Who's the loudest gossip under the sea?

THE BIG-MOUTH CLAM!

Why do oysters give great advice?

THEY HAVE MANY PEARLS OF WISDOM!

Why did the oyster go to the dentist?

HE NEEDED TO GET HIS PEARLY WHITES CLEANED!

Why couldn't the boy mollusk talk to the girl mollusk?

HE KEPT CLAMMING UP!

What happened when Becky ate bad shellfish?

SHE FELT CLAMMY!

Is Becky always this crazy?

YES,
SHE'S A REAL LOON!

What's the most positive seabird?
THE PEL-*I*-CAN!

What game does Hank the septopus like best?

TAG!

Why does Hank make a great crossing guard?

HE CAN HOLD EVERYONE'S HAND!

Where do king crabs live?

IN SAND CASTLES!

How did Dory know that her
bad day would get better?

THE TIDE HAD TURNED!

Who is the loneliest fish?

THE SOLE!

What's Dory's favorite flower?

THE FORGET-ME-NOT!

How do you know Marlin is scared of flying with Becky?

HE
GETS *PAIL!*

Why were the blue tangs in Quarantine?

THEY GOT SEASICK!

Why was the catfish sneezing so much?

HE WAS SICK AS A DOG!

Why do people think Destiny is crazy?

BECAUSE SHE'S A
LITTLE OFF-BALANCE!

How did the hammerhead shark do at his audition?

HE NAILED IT!

How did Bailey and Destiny get out of the tank?

THEY POOLED THEIR TALENTS!

What did the whale shark say when she accepted the truth about herself?

"WHALE, WHALE, WHALE, I GUESS I AM A SHARK."

Why are the sea lions, Fluke and Rudder, so lazy?

THEY'RE ALWAYS LION AROUND!

What is Fluke and Rudder's favorite ice cream flavor?

ROCKY ROAD!

What does Gerald have for lunch at the beach?

SANDWICHES!

What did Fluke and Rudder say when Becky dropped Marlin and Nemo?

"SHE DIDN'T DO IT ON *PORPOISE*!"

What card game do the baby otters love to play?

GO FISH!

Why is Dory so tired?

BECAUSE SHE JUST
KEEPS SWIMMING!

What is the giant squid's favorite type of candy?

A SUCKER!

Why was the mama fish worried about her guppy?

SHE THOUGHT HE'D
BEEN *SQUID*-NAPPED!

Who is the poorest sea creature?

THE URCHIN!

What did the sea cucumber say in the touch pool?

"I'M IN QUITE A PICKLE."

Why did the boy reach into the touch pool?

TO GIVE THE FISH A HAND!

What instinct tells Hank to hide?

HE GETS AN *INKLING* THAT DANGER IS CLOSE!

How does Hank avoid awkward situations?

BY BLENDING IN!

How did the giant squid make the baby squid laugh?

WITH HIS TEN-TICKLES!

Why didn't the squid want to use a pencil?

HE PREFERRED INK!

Why did Squirt tell on Nemo?

HE WAS BEING A LITTLE *TURTLE*-TALE!

Why wasn't Crush worried about the storm?

HE WAS ALWAYS NEAR *SHELL*-TER!

What does Squirt think about migration?

IT IS *TURTLE*-LY AWESOME!

How does Dory stop traffic?

WITH SOMETHING OTTER-LY ADORABLE!

Why did Dory tell Hank to turn the truck around?

BECAUSE THEY NEEDED TO GO IN THE *OTTER* DIRECTION!

Which fish is a carpenter's best friend?

A SAWFISH!

Which fish is a pirate's best friend?

A PARROT FISH!

Which fish is a millionaire's best friend?

A GOLDFISH!

Who is the funniest fish in the sea?

A CLOWN FISH!

What goes on top of an undersea dessert?

CURRENTS!

What did Nemo bake
Dory for her birthday?

A *KELP*-CAKE!

Why didn't Nemo like his dinner?

HE'S A *FINICKY* EATER!

Which fish has the shortest temper?

THE SNAPPER!

Which fish has the deepest voice?

THE SEA BASS!

Which sea creature cries the loudest?

THE *WHALE*!

Why didn't Nemo play ocean football?

HE DIDN'T WANT TO GET *TACKLED!*

Why didn't the sailor's radio work?

IT WAS ON THE WRONG WAVELENGTH!

Did you hear about the mermaid
who married the fisherman?

**SHE FELL FOR HIM
HOOK, LINE, AND SINKER!**

What do you wear to an undersea wedding?

A WET SUIT!

How do you catch a fish with a computer?

**YOU USE THE
INTERNET!**

How do you compliment a catfish?

**TELL HER SHE
LOOKS *PURR*-FECT!**

How do you pay for things at the beach?

WITH SAND DOLLARS!

What did the beach ask the tide?

"WHY ARE YOU ALWAYS GOING OUT WITHOUT ME?"

How does the sea say goodbye?

WITH A WAVE!

Why did Nemo get in trouble?

HE WAS CLOWNING
AROUND!

Why did the fish go to jail?

HE WAS *GILL*-TY!

Who is the saddest creature in the sea?

A *BLUE* WHALE!

Why didn't the baby fish want to leave home?

SHE LIKED BEING COD-DLED!

What did the catfish say when it got hurt?

ME-OWWW!

Why did Nemo take his exam on the surface?

HE THOUGHT IT WOULD
RAISE HIS SEA AVERAGE!

Why do fish live in schools?

BECAUSE THEY'RE SO-*FISH*-TICATED!

Why did Nemo and his friends go to the museum?

FOR A SCHOOL TRIP!

Why did Mr. Ray listen to the swordfish?

HE COULD SEE HIS POINT!

What did Marlin's doctor do when he couldn't make Marlin feel better?

HE SENT HIM TO A STURGEON!

How does an electric eel stay popular?

BY KEEPING CURRENT!

Did you hear about the fish with two eyes on the same side?

HE WAS A FLUKE OF NATURE!

What kind of fish does a cowboy ride?

A SEA HORSE!

What do you call a fish who's falling all over?

A FLOUNDER!

Why was the pilot fish such a great model?

**SHE KNEW HOW TO
WORK A RUNWAY!**

Why was the flying fish so stuck up?

HE ALWAYS HAD HIS NOSE IN THE AIR!

What do people say about the shy sea turtle?

"HE REALLY NEEDS
TO COME OUT OF
HIS SHELL!"

What happened when the wild fish was put in a tank?

HE FLIPPED OUT!

Why don't jellyfish make good liars?

BECAUSE YOU CAN SEE RIGHT THROUGH THEM!

Why was the jellyfish so upset?

HE FOUND HIMSELF IN A JAM!

What did Dory say to Marlin?

"TANKS FOR THE MEMORIES!"

How do crabs avoid danger?

BY SIDESTEPPING IT!

MARLIN: DO YOU SEE ANY FLOWERS IN THE UNDERWATER GARDEN?

DORY: NO, I ONLY *SEAWEED!*

What's the best part of a seafood pizza?

THE *CRUSTACEAN!*

If fish had feet, what kind of shoes would they wear?

FLIP-FLOPS!

Why did Mr. Ray give Marlin 50 clams?

HE NEEDED CHANGE FOR A SAND DOLLAR!

Why don't dogfish and catfish get along?

BECAUSE THEY'RE FROM RIVAL SCHOOLS!

Did you hear about the old, toothless dogfish?

HIS BARK WAS WORSE THAN HIS BITE!

Why couldn't the sea horse sing?

HE WAS A LITTLE HOARSE!

Why did the killer whale want to play the tuba?

SO SHE COULD JOIN THE *ORCA*-STRA!

Why couldn't Hank finish writing his letter?

HE RAN OUT OF INK!

What do you get when you mix a toy with a fish?

A *DOLL*-FIN!

Did you hear about the fish politician?

HE FLIP-FLOPS ON EVERYTHING!

Why don't fish play tennis?

THEY'RE AFRAID OF THE NETS!

How did Dory feel about reuniting with her parents?

SHE WAS ON *FINS* AND NEEDLES!

Where did Charlie and Jenny go on their first date?

THE DIVE-IN!

Why did the sea horse bring Jenny and Charlie a pie?

HE WAS BEING *NEIGH*-BORLY!

Where do Charlie and Jenny sleep?

ON A SEABED!

What do you get when you put two cuttlefish together?

LOTS OF HUGS!

Limericks

There once was a sea lion named **RUDDER**,
Who wished and wished for a **BROTHER**.
And then he met **FLUKE**
(Who was a real **KOOK**).
Now they're so glad they have **EACH OTHER**!

You must meet this gal, **DESTINY**.
She looks like a whale, **DOESN'T SHE?**
Turns out she's a **SHARK**,
And in kind of a **LARK**.
She's a whale shark, and sweet as can **BE!**

There once was a septopus named HANK,
Who escaped from every TANK.
Sad was his STORY
Until he met DORY—
It's her who he'd like to THANK.

There once was a little blue TANG,
Who sang and sang and SANG.
She just kept SWIMMING
(And swimming and SWIMMING),
And that's how she found her whole GANG.

Bailey's a beluga WHALE
With a "condition" that's left him so FRAIL.
His head is a MESS,
But who would have GUESSED
That he'd buck up—jump out—and PREVAIL!

Mr. Ray knows right from **WRONG**.
His lessons are taught with **SONG**.
When Dory comes **BY**
With a gleam in her **EYE**,
He knows that she'll sing **ALONG**!

That Becky was really a **LOON**,
Who imprinted with Marlin so **SOON**!
She took to the **SKY**
(Who knew fish could **FLY**?)—
Their meeting was so **OPPORTUNE**!

Knock-Knock Jokes

KNOCK-KNOCK.
Who's there?
COD.
Cod who?
COD YA RED-HANDED!

Dory: **KNOCK-KNOCK.**
Marlin: Who's there?
Dory: **ER . . . I CAN'T REMEMBER!**

KNOCK-KNOCK.
Who's there?
TAD.
Tad who?
TAD-AAAA!

KNOCK-KNOCK.
Who's there?
DOOYA.
Dooya who?
DOOYA **KNOW THE WAY TO**
THE MARINE LIFE INSTITUTE?

KNOCK-KNOCK.
Who's there?
ANN.
Ann who?
ANN-CHOVY!

KNOCK-KNOCK.
Who's there?
OTTER.
Otter who?
OTTER KNOW. I FORGOT.

KNOCK-KNOCK.
Who's there?
HANK.
Hank who?
HANK **YOU FOR OPENING THE DOOR!**

KNOCK-KNOCK.
Who's there?
WHO'S A FRED.
Who's a Fred who?
WHO'S A-*FRED* OF SHARKS?

KNOCK-KNOCK.
Who's there?
GOBY.
Goby who?
GOBY A DEAR AND LET ME IN!

KNOCK-KNOCK.
Who's there?
MINNOW.
Minnow who?
**NOT SURE, BUT IF YOU FIGURE IT OUT,
LET *MINNOW*.**